Contempt of Court

by

David Landau

Music & Lyrics by

Nikki Stern

A SAMUEL FRENCH ACTING EDITION

SAMUEL FRENCH

FOUNDED 1830

NEW YORK HOLLYWOOD LONDON TORONTO

SAMUELFRENCH.COM

No one shall commit or authorize any act or omission by which the copyright of, or the right to copyright, this play may be impaired.

No one shall make any changes in this play for the purpose of production.

Publication of this play does not imply availability for performance. Both amateurs and professionals considering a production are strongly advised in their own interests to apply to Samuel French, Inc., for written permission before starting rehearsals, advertising, or booking a theatre.

No part of this book may be reproduced, stored in a retrieval system, or transmitted in any form, by any means, now known or yet to be invented, including mechanical, electronic, photocopying, recording, videotaping, or otherwise, without the prior written permission of the publisher.

MUSIC USE NOTE

Licensees are solely responsible for obtaining formal written permission from copyright owners to use copyrighted music in the performance of this play and are strongly cautioned to do so. If no such permission is obtained by the licensee, then the licensee must use only original music that the licensee owns and controls. Licensees are solely responsible and liable for all music clearances and shall indemnify the copyright owners of the play and their licensing agent, Samuel French, Inc., against any costs, expenses, losses and liabilities arising from the use of music by licensees.

IMPORTANT BILLING AND CREDIT
REQUIREMENTS

All producers of *CONTEMPT OF COURT must* give credit to the Author of the Play in all programs distributed in connection with performances of the Play, and in all instances in which the title of the Play appears for the purposes of advertising, publicizing or otherwise exploiting the Play and/ or a production. The name of the Author *must* appear on a separate line on which no other name appears, immediately following the title and *must* appear in size of type not less than fifty percent of the size of the title type.

CONTEMPT OF COURT was first produced under the title *COMEDY COURT*, opening in April 2000 at the Murder To Go Dinner Theatre in Fairfield, NJ under the direction of Bob Lowy with the following cast;

MELISSA CHEATHAM . . . . Kari Schultz
SYDNEY SCHYSTER . . . . Brain Dowd
OFFICE MONDHILL . . . . Mark Bedgood
JUDGE JUDY KOCK . . . . Gayle Hendricks
SNITCH/SIMON/ULGA/ETC. . . . . Peter Timony

CAST

DUKE MONDHILL . . . . Court officer. Dressed in a police uniform. He does check-in.

SYDNEY SCHYSTER . . . . Lawyer with Springer, Schyster & Shark

MELISSA CHEATHAM . . . . Lawyer with Dewy, Cheatham & Howe

JUDGE JUDY KOCH . . . . The honorable Judge Judy

SNITCH/MAN / **RICHARD SIMON** / **DELIVERY BOY** / **NURSE INGA** / **HOWARD COSTAR JR**. . . . . Same actor

SET

There are two tables for the attorneys on either side of the space. Center is a make-shift judge's bench with a chair and beside it a make-shift witness stand, with a short piece of railing in front of it.

NOTES

This is an interactive comedy show wherein the audience serves as jury at several civil cases and actually votes on who wins. Upon entering the audience receives a program in the form of a Jury Duty Summons. Inside the program should be the Juror Ballots with four places to write answers one for each case. The program reads:

"Good evening Ladies and Gentlemen and thank you for answering your summons for Jury Duty at the funniest Peoples Night Court. Tonight, not only will you decide the outcome of the four most comical cases of the century (by using the juror ballots enclosed), but some of you will be called upon as plaintiffs, defendants, even witnesses as you serve in CONTEMPT OF COURT."

Audience members are greeted by Officer Mondhill - the court officer. They are seated by the attorneys, who recognize patrons as people they represented or sued or attempt to solicit business from by handing out business cards. The two attorneys and Duke will walk-around and greet people, selecting for themselves who they might call on in the scenes to come.

This script is meant to be performed in the fast and flippant style of the Marx brothers – especially the two lawyers, with the Judge as the straight woman.

NOTES ON PRODUCTION

PERFORMANCE SPACE

The following play was designed to be performed in almost any performance space, from a theater to a dining room, dinner theater, night club, theater-in-the-round, or a thrust stage where the acting area is level with the first row. The performance is a sort of reverse theater in the round, with action performed around the circumference of the seating area, as well as down the aisles and in the center. The audience could be seated at tables, either dinner or cocktail for dinner theater or night club/cabaret productions.

SCENES & BREAKS

The script is formatted into four scenes running in length from 15 to 20 minutes. Between each scene is time for the audience to fill out their Ballot Sheet, as well as to serve a course of a meal, serve drinks, or play music as desired. During these breaks characters mingle helping to establish character and reveal information to the audience in a one on one manner. The script can easily be adapted to shorten or eliminate some of these breaks. But there should be some kind of break just before the final scene to allow audience members to hand in their Ballot Sheets.

MUSICAL NUMBER

The musical number in the show has been designed to be performed to a taped play back. Once a performance license has been secured, an audio tape with recordings of both the instrumentals and the composer singing the lyrics can be obtained from Samuel French. Also on the recording is the opening theme music which is to be used at the beginning of each scene.

For more information contact Samuel French, Inc. at info@samuel-french.com.

Music & Lyrics were composed by Nikki Stern.

ACT 1

(The lights dim. Music plays. **SCHYSTER** *and* **CHEATHAM** *enter, holding hands and carrying their breifcases.)*

SCHYSTER. Huggy bear.

CHEATHAM. Sweetie pie.

SCHYSTER. Yummy buns.

CHEATHAM. Kissy poo.

SCHYSTER. Wasn't last night just –

CHEATHAM. My heart never pounded so fast. You were just so –

SCHYSTER. It was all you, my precious – I was just trying to keep up with you.

CHEATHAM. You're so sweet.

SCHYSTER. It's the things you do to me.

CHEATHAM. To each other.

(They giggle and rub noses as **MONDHILL** *enters and stands center.)*

MONDHILL. Here yea, Here yea, this session of the Peoples Night Court is now in session.

SCHYSTER & CHEATHAM. Time to go to work! Good luck dear.

(They kiss quickly and part to separate sides of the room.)

MONDHILL. The honorable Judge Judy Koch presiding. All rise!

*(***JUDGE,*** in robe, enters and walks to a stool or high directors chair set in front of a podium or music stand. She hits her gavel.)*

JUDGE. You may all be seated.

(*Just as everyone starts to sit down.*)

MONDHILL. All rise. The Judge didn't say Simon says.

(**MONDHILL** *and* **JUDGE** *laugh.*)

JUDGE. Oh, Officer Mondhill, you're such a joker. Simon says you may all be seated.
(*To* **MONDHILL**) So, who do you put your money on tonight?

MONDHILL. Ms. Cheatham. She was smoking last night. I think she has Schyster off balance. I think he'll be going into this round more cautious, giving her the upper hand, which is all she needs to make a clean sweep.

JUDGE. No way, Duke baby. Schyster may have fallen last night, but that makes him all the more likely to strike out hard and make a strong come back. Cheatham's probably going to get herself caught off-guard, still basking in the glow from the last round. My money's on Schyster.

MONDHILL. How much?

JUDGE. One hundred. (*She pulls out cash*)

MONDHILL. One hundred? Are you sure?

JUDGE. It's time to put up or shut up.

MONDHILL. (*Pulling out cash*) This will be like taking a card from an ambulance chaser. You've got yourself a bet.

(*He puts the money under the wooden base for the gavel. The* **JUDGE** *takes the gavel and strikes it three times.*)

MONDHILL. This court will now come to order.

JUDGE. Ladies and Gentlemen, thank you for answering your summons to appear tonight for Jury Duty. Yes, we know you thought you were just going out for a fun dinner theater show like one of those murder mysteries or that silly wedding thing – Tommy and Tinkerbell's – whatever. But in actuality, you were just served genuine summons when you arrived here tonight. You see, with so many people coming up with the most ridiculous excuses to get out of jury duty, New Jersey State (*or name of whatever State the show is in*) has initiated a new pilot program called People's Night Court. The only way the State has come up with to collect a qualified jury of the defendant's peers is by tricking the public into showing up. The best part of this program is that the ticket price you paid will go to off-set the programs cost. And that is why we have done away with the jury of twelve and opened it up to as many as we can pack into a dining room at one time.

MONDHILL. It also makes it more fun.

JUDGE. Now, the cases you will hear and ultimately decide upon tonight are not criminal, but civil cases. Thus, only a majority is required to decide a case. I am the judge of the law. But you, ladies and gentlemen, will be the judge of these cases. At the conclusion of arguments presented by the plaintiff and the defendant's attorneys, YOU – as jurors – will deliberate between cases and shall determine the outcome of the case by voting with the appropiate juror ballot sheet provided and handing them in to Court Officer Mondhill. If you have any questions, that's too damn bad, because the State only has the hall rented for three hours. So, without further delay, Officer Mondhill, the first case please.

MONDHILL. Ah, there's a slight problem, your honor.

JUDGE. What's that?

MONDHILL. The court stenographer just had an allergic reaction to the perfume of someone else at the table and had to be sent home.

JUDGE. Well, pick another one from the jury pool.

(**MONDHILL** *selects a person from the audience and gives them a steno pad and a pencil. He instructs them to keep good notes and adlibs a quick swearing in, such as reciting the alphabet.*)

JUDGE. Now that that's settled, present the first case.

MONDHILL. Ah, your honor? There's also the matter of the court artist. The state wouldn't spring for the overtime.

JUDGE. Typical of Governor Whitman (*whoever the governor is*). Okay, pick some one else from the jury pool.

(**MONDHILL** *selects a person and gives them a sketch pad and pencil.*)

JUDGE. Now, can we proceed with the first case?

MONDHILL. Fandangelmen vs Guffman, medical malpractice. One million dollars in damages being sought by Fandangelmen, $250,000 being sought by Guffman in countersuit. Attorney for the plaintiff Mr.Schyster, attorney for the defendant Ms.Cheatham.

JUDGE. Mr. Shyster, are you ready to proceed?

SCHYSTER. Yes your honor. (*Standing up to face the crowd*) Ladies and gentlemen, which is only about three of you, and all the rest of the jury. What you are about to hear is a story of heartbreak and betrayal, of medical science gone astray, of incredible negligence and unbelievable audacity – which is my opening statement. How many of you put off going to the doctor as long as possible? I know I do, which may explain the fact that my hemorrhoids now receive more mail than I do. And why is that? They have more friends. But lets get back to going to doctors. Or, lets get back to not going to doctors and save ourselves a lot of money. There is no question that one reason we resist going to the doctor is those outrageous medical fees and needless tests we are constantly subjected to. Which is actually two reasons, and lets not forget the embarrassment of having to take our clothes off and put on that flimsy, translucent tissue paper robe that tears the second you try to put it on and leaves your backside open for the entire waiting room to see when the doctor walks in.

JUDGE. (*to* **MONDHILL**) See how fast he's coming out swinging?

MONDHILL. He's right about those robes – and the hemorrhoids –

JUDGE. Shhh.

SCHYSTER. No, Ladies and Gentleman and everyone in between, it is not these that make us hesitate in seeking medical attention, although it should be. It is the total loss of confidence we have gained over the years in a medical profession that has been brought before these very courts time and time again for malpractice and total disregard for we, the patients?

CHEATHAM. Objection your honor. Over acting.

JUDGE. Sustained. Get to the point, counselor.

SCHYSTER. The point?

JUDGE. You do have a point, don't you?

SCHYSTER. Of course not, I'm a lawyer. But now you've made me lose my place.

CHEATHAM. Well, it's certainly not in a courtroom.

SCHYSTER. Objection, your honor, I resemble that remark.

JUDGE. Sustained. Would you like to have your opening statement read back to you by the court stenographer?

MONDHILL. I'll bet the court stenographer wouldn't.

JUDGE. Yeah, but I'd like to hear her try.

> (**MONDHILL** *has the court stenographer stand and read back whatever she may have written, if anything.*)

MONDHILL. Did you write that short hand or long hand?

> (*It doesn't matter what she answers.*)

MONDHILL. Next time, try both hands.

JUDGE. Now, if the planitiff's Counselor would continue?

SCHYSTER. Hey, I'm not finished yet.

MONDHILL. I think you were finished before you started. You are the counselor for the plaintiff, Mr. Schyster.

SCHYSTER. Oh, right. Who asked you anyway? (*Looks through papers*) Now, where did I leave the point, the point – Oh, here it is. Ladies and Gentlemen of the Jury, and any body else still following this, on the night of March 31st of last year, my client, Carol Dangfangelmen, the plaintiff in this case –

MONDHILL. Fandangelmen.

SCHYSTER. Gasundhieght.

MONDHILL. No, the case filing states the name of the plaintiff as Carol Fandangelman.

SCHYSTER. Isn't that what I said?

MONDHILL, JUDGE, CHEATHAM. Nooo!

CHEATHAM. Your honor, I move to have this case thrown out of court. First not only is it of a highly questionable foundation, but the plaintiff's attorney has put so much weight into the case that he doesn't even know his own client's name.

SCHYSTER. I know the name. I just had a long night last night and Gangfandelman is just not an easy name to remember when you're suffering from a hangover. Even if your not suffering from a hang-over, for that matter..

MONDHILL, JUDGE, CHEATHAM. Fangdangelmen!

SCHYSTER. Lets not be so picky.

JUDGE. Mr. Schyster, if you had a long night last night, it still does not explain you having a hangover at this time of night tonight.

SCHYSTER. Last night just ended an hour ago, your honor.

JUDGE. I sincerely hope you have not been drinking before entering my courtroom. You know what I think of lawyers who drink before entering my courtroom?

SCHYSTER. I know all lawyers think about drinking after leaving your courtroom, your honor.

(**MONDHILL & CHEATHAM** *laugh.*)

JUDGE. (*Hits gavel*) Another crack like that and I'll hold you in contempt of court.

SCHYSTER. You can hold me any where you'd like Judge.

JUDGE. Mr. Schyster, you try my patience.

SCHYSTER. Why, thank you, you honor – and you should try mine sometimes. But right now it's a patient of Doctor Guffman over there that has been very trying – trying to get justice from this Doctor Guffman, if this Dr. Guffman really is a doctor – as if any credible institute of higher learning would ever give a diploma to someone with a name like that.

CHEATHAM. Why not. They gave one to someone with the name of Shyster.

SCHYSTER. They certainly did not! I got mine through the inside of a matchbook cover, like everyone else in the legal profession. But it was under the cover of darkness that my client, Carol – you know – the plaintiff over here (*to an attractive woman in audience*) Madam would you stand up for a moment?

(*Hopefully, she will stand up.*)

SCHYSTER. It was a harsh and wind swept night that my client went into Doctor Guffman's office for emergency treatment of an excruciatingly painful but routine urinary problem and came out like this! (*He slams the table*) Sure, a beautiful woman you say, but hardly the man she once was – hardly the Mister Carol Dangfangelmen that went into that office before a drunken, incompetent doctor put a scalpel to her – him – whatever. For on April 1st Carol FangDangGangelmang woke up looking like this (*points to woman*) instead of this (*holds up a photo of a sloppy ugly man*).

MONDHILL. (*To* **JUDGE**) Not bad.

JUDGE. Get this doctors number. My aunt Tilly wants another face lift. She's already had three and she still looks like Ronald Reagan.

SCHYSTER. Okay, maybe a decided improvement, but hardly what the doctor ordered. Or at least not what the patient ordered. This is a clear and obvious case of medical malfeasance, whatever that really means, and overwhelmingly entitles my client to compensatory damages for mental anguish, not to mention having to buy a whole new wardrobe. I know you'll agree with me that one million dollars is a fair and equitable fee – especially as I'll get a third. Thank you. (*To* **WOMAN**) You may be seated Carol. I know how hard this is for you, but justice will be done and we'll make a mint.

(*He winks at her*)

JUDGE. Thank you, Mr. Shyster, I think. Counselor Cheatham, is the defense ready to present opening remarks?

CHEATHAM. Yes, your honor. (*She stands*) Ladies and Gentlemen of the Jury –

SCHYSTER. Objection!

CHEATHAM. To what?

SCHYSTER. To that man's tie over there.

JUDGE. (*Slamming gavel*) Mr. Schyster, you must contain yourself to the legal procedures of this court and not to extraneous remarks about some man's (*turning to look at the man pointed out, and suddenly looks shocked*) yuch! – Sir, if I ever see you wearing that tie again, I'll fine you in contempt of court. Objection sustained. (*Hits gavel*) The defense may continue.

CHEATHAM. Thank you, your honor. Ladies and Gentlemen of the Jury, your honor, people of the court – I hope that covers everyone – My client, (*She pats a patron on the shoulder*) Dr. Guffman, may not have the cleanest of records in his medical career. Yes, he may have been expelled from some of the lowest of medical institutions, fired from three third world country hospitals and found mentally incompetent to stand trial in a jaywalking case, but it was not his consistent state of inebriation nor his addictive dependency on nitrous oxide that resulted in his performing a sex adjustment operation to the plaintiff on the night in question – No! (*She slams a table*)

SCHYSTER. (*Surprised*) It wasn't?

(**CHEATHAM** *looks suddenly unsure. She quickly checks her notes, then exhales relieved.*)

CHEATHAM. No – it was circumstance.

SCHYSTER. (*to his client*) Well, we'll sue this Sir Cumstance later. But right now it's Dr. Guffman we're after.

CHEATHAM. The defense will show that on the night of March 31st of last year, the plaintiff, going under the fictitious name of Fandangelmen, rushed in to the medical clinic building that my client Dr. Guffman had illegally set up practice in, as he does not have a license to practice medicine in this state, not due to a painful urinary infection as the plaintiff's slipshod and incompetent attorney contends – No ladies and gentlemen, but because this plaintiff, this man sitting right there (*pointing to woman client*) was a fugitive from the law in desperate need of a new identity. And in the same building, on the same floor, right next door to my client's office in fact, is the office of another less than reputable medical practitioner who happens to specialize in one hour plastic surgery for those in the criminal profession. And this doctor happens to also bear the name of Doctor Guffman.

MONDHILL. Impossible!

JUDGE. Unless they're brothers or something.

MONDHILL. Not a chance.

CHEATHAM. As a matter of fact they are, fraternal twins – different mothers – but that's immaterial to the case.

(**JUDGE** *snaps her fingers and* **MONDHILL** *pays her ten bucks.*)

JUDGE. The defense may continue.

CHEATHAM. Ladies and gentlemen, put yourselves in the place of my client. You have just finished a grueling day of man handling sexual organs – I mean transplanting – and you are setting back to finish off your second bottle of vermouth after taking a long and suffocating whiff of nitrous oxide when in through the door bursts this horribly dangerous looking man, who addresses you by name, points a gun at you and then demands that you, and I quote, "change me, make me someone new." If you, ladies and gentlemen of the jury, were my client and found yourself in the same circumstances, there is no doubt that you would have acted the same. There is certainly no basis for a case of malpractice. More over, my client has never been paid for his skilled services rendered to the plaintiff and as the plaintiff has sold the rights to her story to Fox Television as a Movie of the Week for the sum of one million dollars, my client is certainly due his fee plus a percentage of the million dollar movie deal. Thank you.

MONDHILL. A Million dollars. (*Whistles*)

SCHYSTER. One million dollars! (*Standing*) Your honor, the counsel for the plaintiff would like to move for a short recess to renegotiate his fee.

JUDGE. Motion denied. (*Slams gavel*) Mr. Shyster, are you ready to call your first witness?

SCHYSTER. No, but that's never stopped me before. The plaintiff would like to call Mr. Symore the Snitch to the stand.

MONDHILL. Mr. Snitch?

(**SNITCH**, *dressed like a thug, enters and takes the stand.* **MONDHILL** *approaches him and immediately* **SNITCH** *turns around and places his hands on the wall ready to be searched and arrested.*)

JUDGE. No, Mr. Snitch, you're just being sworn in.

SNITCH. You sure?

MONDHILL. Yes. Now if you would turn around please so I can swear you in?

SNITCH. (*Turning around*) Sorry, it's just something I also seem to do every time I see a cop uniform. It's a natural reflex.

MONDHILL. No doubt. Please place your left hand on the bible and raise your right.

(**SNITCH** *starts to, but can't decide which hand to place on the bible and which to raise, alternating back and forth and back and forth.* **MONDHILL** *is getting irritated.*)

MONDHILL. Just pick one!

(**SNITCH** *stops.*)

MONDHILL. Do you solemnly swear to tell the truth, the whole truth and nothing but the truth so help you God?

SNITCH. What exactly do you mean by the truth?

MONDHILL. Just sit down.

SCHYSTER. Mr. Snitch. You are a close associate of Mr. Carol Fangdangelmen, are you not?

SNITCH. Not no more we ain't. Since he's turned into a regular babe he ain't got time for those of us who were his pals when he was nothing but a gutter snake.

SCHYSTER. But were you with the plaintiff on the night in question?

SNITCH. The who when?

JUDGE. I think what the counselor is getting at, Mr. Snitch, is whether you were with Carol the night he got his sex change operation?

SNITCH. Oh, sure thing. We was just got out of the slammer – having wriggled through that tunnel we'd been diggin for the past three years, Like this –

(*As he says this he wiggles out through the railing of the witness stand and makes a run for it, but* **MONDHILL** *grabs him and brings him back.*)

SNITCH. and we was on the run and we knows of this doctor named Guffman that some of the boys in the pen had told us about that did this plastical sturdgerey so's the coppers can't recognoyter yous no more. So we gets to da the medical building type place and run into the first office we see that's got the monkeier Guffman on the door and we're looking for the bathroom cause we both gotta go like race horses on obitchuatesl.

SCHYSTER. You were both suffering urinary pain?

SNITCH. Like you wouldn't believe. Carol says he hurts so bad its worser than the time he hid out in a beer Factory.

JUDGE. Thank you, go on Mr. Snitch.

SNITCH. Well, that's when we see the doctor.

SCHYSTER. And is that doctor in the courtroom tonight?

SNITCH. Sure he is, he's that guy right over there. I recognoyter him even thoses he's sober.

SCHYSTER. And was he sober when you first met him that fateful night?

SNITCH. I thought it was a night in March actually, but the doc sure weren't sober – he was smashed to the gils and gigglin a lot. We asked him if he was the Dr. Guffman that changes people in a rush and he says he is and Carol goes first, cause he was much more, how you say, aggressiontory like than I was. So's the doc gives Carol a whiff of this gas and then takes a few whiffs for himself and then he starts to go at it and I pass out right then and there on the floor.

SCHYSTER. Did the doctor have Carol sign any permits, authorization forms, medical notifications or even explain what he was going to do prior to starting the surgery?

SNITCH. Nawh, he was too hyped up on that gas stuff. He just tosses Carol down on the table and shoves the gas mask cup thing in his face and then gives Carol a punch in the stomach so's Carol has to suck in a deep breath of the gas stuff and then clocks out, bam, like that. The next thing I know I wakes up in the morning and the docs out cold with the gas mask cup thing on his mouth and there on the table is this babe where Carol used to be.

SCHYSTER. And is this babe in the courtroom this evening?

SNITCH. You got problems with your eyes Mister? You know she is. She's your client. That's her sittin right over there. Maybe you should otta get you some of them there glass bottle trifocals or somethin.

SCHYSTER. And when Carol awoke to discover himself a herself, what was his – her reaction.

SNITCH. It took me all my strength to hold him – her back from killin the passed out doc.

SCHYSTER. In other words he wasn't pleased with his new look?

CHEATHAM. Objection, your honor – leading the witness.

JUDGE. Sustained. Court stenographer, strike that from the record.

MONDHILL. (*Looking over the stenographer's shoulder*) I don't think she's gottin that far yet.

SCHYSTER. I'll rephrase the question. Did he say why he wanted to kill the passed out doc?

SNITCH. Sure, he says all he wanted was a different face, not to lose his manhood.

SCHYSTER. Not to lose his manhood. How eloquently said. No further questions your honor.

JUDGE. Does the defense wish to cross examine?

CHEATHAM. Yes, your honor. Mr. Snitch, at any time prior to the operation did Carol Fangdangelmen ever tell Doctor Guffman that the only thing he wanted changed was his face?

SNITCH. Well, no –

CHEATHAM. So the only things the plaintiff did ask of the doctor was whether his name was Guffman and then to ask to be changed, is that correct?

SNITCH. Well, first we asked where the john was, cause we had to go so bad after holding it in since we crashed out of the slammer and all.

CHEATHAM. Did the doctor ever say he would only change the plaintiffs face?

SNITCH. Nawh, the doc there didn't say nothing cept a belch and a burp or two. Never said a word, just dug right in, cuttin away and all.

(*All the men squirm.*)

CHEATHAM. You said that the next morning when the plaintiff discovers himself to be a woman he was upset to the point of attempting to kill the sleeping doctor.

SNITCH. That's right.

CHEATHAM. Did the plaintiff ever pay the doctor – with a credit card before the operation or leave a check or cash after the operation?

SNITCH. Are you nutty? Course not. Didn't pay the drunken loser a red or any other color penny.

CHEATHAM. The last time you spoke with the plaintiff, Carol Fandangelman, did she tell you anything about her movie deal?

SNITCH. Sure did. Said that doctorin was turning into the best damn scam yet. Made me wish I had gone ahead and done it.

CHEATHAM. Done what? Lost your manhood? Would that be worth one million dollars to you?

SNITCH. Well – I – I object!

MONDHILL. Sorry to interrupt, counselor, your honor – (*handcuffing* **SNITCH**) but Mr. Snitch here is only on a very short time furlough from the state prison and must now be returned to custody.

SNITCH. I object to that too.

CHEATHAM. That's alright, officer, the defense has no further questions.

JUDGE. Very well, the witness is excused.

> (**MONDHILL** *escorts* **SNITCH** *out the door. As he does, both lawyers rush up to give him their cards to represent his case. The* **JUDGE** *slams the gavel. The two lawyers rush back to their places.*)

JUDGE. Does the plaintiff have any further witnesses, counselor?

SCHYSTER. No, your honor. The plaintiff rests. And that's the problem. The plaintiffs always resting while we do all the hard work. And we only get a third.

JUDGE. Thank you, Mr. Schyster. Ms. Cheatham, does the defense wish to call any witnessess?

CHEATHAM. No, your honor.

JUDGE. Not even Doctor Guffman himself?

CHEATHAM. I'm afraid he's unfit to take the stand, just look at him.

JUDGE. Ugh, you're right. Very well. Mr. Schyster, the plaintiffs closing statement?

SCHYSTER. Right. Ladies and gentlemen of the Jury, under the law it doesn't matter what a persons past is or what luck they may have encountered afterwards. What matters is that my client went into a doctors office wishing to use the bathroom and came out not knowing which public restroom to use in the future. If you walk into a hair salon and ask for a new look, that does not give the stylist the right to hack away and make you bald. Some things, especially the taking away of one's manhood, require permission, at least verbal if not written. No such permission was given to Doctor Guffman to perform the operation he performed. I ask that you find the defendant guilty and award me my hard earned one third commission. I haven't won a case in a month and I'm behind in my rent. Thank you.

JUDGE. Thank you, Mr. Schyster. Ms. Cheatham, the defense's closing statement.

CHEATHAM. Thank you, your honor. Ladies and gentlemen of the Jury, as the plaintiffs attorney said, under the law it doesn't matter one's past. Doctor Guffman did exactly what was requested of him by the plaintiff, within the confines of his normal practice. Nothing more and nothing less. It was not my client's fault that the plaintiff entered the wrong doctors office. Obviously my clients work was so successful that the plaintiff has already made substantial financial gains from it and yet my client, Doctor Guffman, has received nothing for his labors and skills. I ask that you find in favor of giving the doctor his due. After all, with a one million dollar TV movie deal, the plaintiff can easy afford to pay my commission as well. Thank you.

JUDGE. Thank you, Ms. Cheatham. And now, ladies and gentlemen of the jury, the time has come for you to deliberate the merits of both sides of this case over the next break. I ask that you make your decision by marking your juror ballot sheet for Case 1: Fangdangelmen

VS Guffman. Final judgements on all cases heard tonight will be at the conclusion of the session. Thank you and good deliberating.

(*The* **JUDGE** *hits the gavel. Short break as the next course is served, if dinner theater. The two attorneys walk around and attempt to persuade the jurors.*)

ACT II

(Lights go down and come back up with music. The two lawyers stand as the JUDGE enters.)

MONDHILL. Here yea, here yea, this court is now back in session, Her honorable Judge Judy Koch presiding. All rise – all be seated.

JUDGE. Thank you, Officer Mondhill.

MONDHILL. Don't mention it Judge, just doing my job. Speaking of which, as I know the press will be very interested in the proceedings this evening, I thought we might take this opportunity to see some of the fine sketches done by our court artist.

JUDGE. That's a grand idea. Bring out the sketches. A little art is always good for the soul.

*(**MONDHILL** holds up the sketches. Everyone reacts [probably disappointed, unless they've happened to pick a good artist])*

JUDGE. And that's a little art alright. Very little.

MONDHILL. Perhaps it's time to solicit a new artist?

*(The **JUDGE** nods and **MONDHILL** selects a new artist.)*

JUDGE. Shall we proceed with the next case, Officer Mondhill?

MONDHILL. Yes, your honor, however I think we may wish to solicit a new court stenographer as well. The last one is suffering from writers cramp and she's still on the opening statements.

JUDGE. Select away, Mondhill.

*(**MONDHILL** selects a new court stenographer, giving them the steno pad and pencil and adlibbing some kind of swearing in.)*

JUDGE. Aptly done, Officer. Now, the next case on the docket, if you please?

MONDHILL. Mrs. Winifred Belmore versus McDuffs Fast Burger for reckless endangerment. Attorney for plaintiff Ms. Cheatham, attorney for defendant Mr. Schyster.

JUDGE. So entered. Is plaintiff's attorney ready for opening statements?

CHEATHAM. Yes, your honor. It was a cold and frigid winter morning when my unsuspecting client, Winifred Belmore (*gesturing to a gentle looking older woman in the audience*), left the drive through window of her favorite Scottish fast food restaurant with the Loch Ness scrambled eggs and banger breakfast for herself and seventeen venison McNugget happy meals which she acquired to distribute to a family of orphans from Absentgarberstan. Worried about the orphans possible malnutrition and behind schedule for her appointment at Sister Susies Sharpened Nail Salon, Mrs. Belmore placed the cup of coffee that was an essential part of her breakfast between her knees to steady it as she removed from the happy meals the teanie beanie baby toys that can be resold for a considerable sum on the collectors market and talked on her cell phone all while skillfully piloting her leased Lexus around those annoying yellow school buses with their blinking red lights that kept stopping and interfering with her maintaining her cruising speed of 65 miles an hour on a 35 mile a hour marked residential streets. Little did she know that what she thought was an innocent warm beverage placed in her lap was in actuality a highly dangerous potentially lethal scolding hot time boom. For as she side swiped a driver training vehicle and made a sharp 90 degree turn, just beating a one legged 80 year old war veteran into a handicapped parking space, that Styrofoam concealed weapon exploded on her lap – scolding her legs and causing her enormous suffering, not to mention missing her nail appointment.

JUDGE. Wow – those are really hard to get at Sister Susies. You have to book six weeks in advance.

CHEATHAM. Are we, the public consumer, no longer safe from products that are callously placed on the market which can bestow harm and destruction to our lives? Shouldn't these companies that ignore warning labels and safe guards be made to pay for their willful negligence? The plaintiff intends to show that –

(*The* JUDGE *hits her gavel.*)

JUDGE. A moment for clarification.

CHEATHAM. (*Whinning*) But I'll lose my place – .

SCHYSTER. It certaintly isn't in a courtroom.

JUDGE. Is your client suing a fast food establishment because after ordering a hot cup of coffee on a cold winter day she spilled it on her own lap through reckless driving?

CHEATHAM. Of course.

JUDGE. Ms. Cheatham. The American justice system was not put in place so that people might seek financial rewards from their own stupidity.

CHEATHAM & SCHYSTER. It wasn't?

JUDGE. No! This is a court of law, not a publishers clearinghouse sweepstake for those without common sense. I am refusing to hear this case and throwing it out as a waste of the courts time and the tax payers money. Please present us with a case worthy of litigation and not a frivolous and blatant effort to get something for nothing.

CHEATHAM & SCHYSTER. Uh oh.

(*They start going through their papers, desperately reading them, then crumpling them up and throwing them away, shouting out cases*)

CHEATHAM. Woman sues microwave manufacturer after using it as a hair-dryer for her miniature poodle?

SCHYSTER. 90 year old recovering stroke victim sues electric lawnmower company after getting a heart attack trying to pull start the engine?

CHEATHAM. Family sues aquarium park after drug induced son drowns in Killer Whale pool after breaking in late at night?

SCHYSTER. Street bum sues library for throwing him out after defecating on the floor?

CHEATHAM. (*Bursting out crying*) This is futile – we'll never find a civil case that's actually worthy of being tried!

SCHYSTER. (*Dropping to his knees, pleading*) You can't do this to us, your Honor. You'll put us out of business.

JUDGE. I'm not doing anything. It's you lawyers that are to blame, for trying to make everything into a potential law suit.

CHEATHAM. We're to blame?

SCHYSTER. We're to blame?

(*Music "**BLAME THE LAWYERS**"*)

SCHYSTER.

EVER SINCE WILLIAM SHAKESPEARE
SUGGESTED THEY KILL US ALL FIRST

CHEATHAM.

LAWYERS HAVE BEEN MUCH ABUSED

SCHYSTER.

MUCH MALIGNED

JUDGE.

DISRESPECTED

MONDHILL.

DETESTED

SCHYSTER & CHEATHAM.

AND CURSED.

CHEATHAM.

ARE WE ADMIRED AS SCHOLARS?

JUDGE & MONDHILL.

HA

SCHYSTER.

OR PRAISED FOR OUR ORATORY SKILL?

JUDGE & MONDHILL.

NO!

CHEATHAM.

WE'RE BRANDED AS CHARLATANS

SCHYSTER.

SHYSTERS AND SHARKS

JUDGE & MONDHILL.

WHO SMELL BLOOD AND MOVE IN FOR THE KILL

CHEATHAM.

WHY DO YOU

SCHYSTER & CHEATHAM.

BLAME THE LAWYERS

(*They all clap*)

JUDGE & MONDHILL.

BLAME THE LAWYERS

(*They all clap*)

SCHYSTER.

SAY THE JUDGE DENIES BAIL
AND THEY THROW YOU IN JAIL
WHO'S TO BLAME?

CHEATHAM. Not your hard – working attorney!

SCHYSTER.

BUT YOU –

SCHYSTER & CHEATHAM.

BLAME THE LAWYERS

(*They all clap – getting the audience to clap as well.*)

JUDGE & MONDHILL.

BLAME THE LAWYERS

(*They all clap*)

SCHYSTER.

YOU MAY TREAT US LIKE DIRT
BUT THE CRUELTY CAN HURT
ALL THE SAME

CHEATHAM.

WHAT HAVE WE DONE TO DESERVE THIS
I AND MY FELLOW ESQUIRES?

MONDHILL.

IS IT THEIR POWERS?

JUDGE.

OR THE BILLABLE HOURS?

SCHYSTER & CHEATHAM.

WHICH THE LEGAL PROFESSION REQUIRES!

SCHYSTER.

WE'RE JUST THE ONES PUSHING PAPERS
NOT THE ONE TAKING YOUR HOUSE

JUDGE & MONDHILL.

YOU DON'T HOLD IT AGAINST THEM
FOR WINNING THAT SIZABLE SETTLEMENT
FOR YOUR SPOUSE

CHEATHAM.

WHY DO YOU –

SCHYSTER & CHEATHAM.

BLAME THE LAWYERS

(*They all clap*)

JUDGE & MONDHILL.

BLAME THE LAWYERS

(*They all clap*)

SCHYSTER.

HOW DOES IT LOOK
WHEN YOU CALL ME A CROOK
TO MY FACE?

CHEATHAM. What about our reputations?

SCHYSTER.

BUT YOU STILL –

SCHYSTER & CHEATHAM.

BLAME THE LAWYERS

(*They all clap*)

JUDGE & MONDHILL.

BLAME THE LAWYERS

(*They all clap*)

CHEATHAM.

    DON'T COME LOOKING FOR ME
    AND EXPECT ME TO BE
    ON YOUR CASE.

SCHYSTER.

    NO, WE'RE NOT PERFECT

CHEATHAM.

    WE ALL HAVE OUR FLAWS

JUDGE.

    SO THEY FAILED TO POINT OUT
    THERE WAS ONE LITTLE CLAUSE

MONDHILL.

    MAYBE NOW YOU'RE INDEBTED THE REST OF YOUR
    LIFE

JUDGE.

    AND THEY'VE ALL TURNED AGAINST

MONDHILL.

    INCLUDING YOUR WIFE

ALL.

    TELL US, WHO CAN YOU COUNT ON
    THROUGH THICK AND THROUGH THIN
    TO GET OUT OF THE MESS
    THAT THEY HELPED GET YOU IN
    WHO WILL KEEP YOU IN COURT
    TIL THEY'VE SPENT YOUR LAST DIME?

JUDGE & MONDHILL. It's your faithful attorneys at law.

SCHYSTER & CHEATHAM.

    BOTTOM LINE IS
    DON'T BLAME US
    FOR DOING WHAT WE DO

JUDGE & MONDHILL.

    IF YOU'RE NOT SATISFIED

ALL.

    YOU CAN ALWAYS SUE!

    (After applause – a man bursts in with a gun.)

MAN. It's not true – not a word of it, I tell you. She didn't do anything. It was me – I did it all and no one ever knew. (*Fiendish laugh*) Ha, ha, ha. And I did it because she never paid any attention to me. She never so much as looked at me – if she had even sneezed in my direction, even that would have been something – but Noooooooo –

(*Suddenly he notices everyone staring at him and that it doesn't look like the right courtroom.*)

MAN. Oh – ah – Isn't this Courtroom 123?

MONDHILL. No – Next one down the hall.

MAN. Down the hall – right. Oops – ha – sorry. Just forget I was ever here.

(*He tip toes out.*)

JUDGE. Ms. Cheatham, Mr. Schyster – how often have you two been up before me?

SCHYSTER. I'm not sure, your Honor – what time to you get up?

JUDGE. Mr. Schyster, looking at you I can see why lawyers are always said to be *practicing*. You are the only attorney I know who actually built a saloon in his basement in order to study for his bar exam.

MONDHILL. At least now he's licensed in the state of inebriation.

JUDGE. This court demands that you find us a case worthy of our time or I will hold both of you in contempt of court.

CHEATHAM. I've been held in worse places.

JUDGE. FIND ME A CASE!

(*She slams the gavel. They start to frantically search the portfolios.*)

MONDHILL. You know, I bet I know why it's called legal paper.

JUDGE. Why?

MONDHILL. Because you couldn't fit all that BS on standard 8 1/2 x 11 sheets.

JUDGE. You know, I think you have something there Mondhill.

MONDHILL. (*Feeling his nose embarrased*) Where?

JUDGE. Forget it. (*To the attorneys*) I'm losing my patients.

MONDHILL. My Psychologist lost all hers too – but I think police the found them.

JUDGE. Mondhill, I think you need to get out more.

MONDHILL. Okay.

(*He starts to leave.*)

JUDGE. I didn't mean now, Officer Mondhill.

MONDHILL. (*Coming back*) Right – I knew that.

CHEATHAM. (*Excited*) Wait, wait. I found one – I found one! Docket number 32!

SCHYSTER. Docket number 32? Docket 32 – Docket 32 where are you? (*he finds it*) Got it!

(*They both dash up and hand legal sheets to* **MONDHILL.**)

JUDGE. Officer Mondhill, call case docket number 32!

MONDHILL. Class action suit, represented by Dewy, Cheatham and Howe against the Stardom Talent Agency, represented by Springer, Schyster and Shark, for fraud, misrepresentation and breech of contract. Countersuit by Stardom Talent Agency against the Plaintiffs for libel and defamation of character.

JUDGE. This should be fun. Counselor Cheatham, as you are presenting this class action suit, you have the honors of going first again – don't waste it this time. Your opening statement?

CHEATHAM. (*standing*) Thank you, your honor. Ladies and Gentlemen of the jury, my firm has been selected to represent the interests of these fine individuals (Points to three tables) –

SCHYSTER. Objection. (*Motions to table*) Fine individuals? Just look at them!

JUDGE. Point, Mr. Schyster. Objection Sustained. Counsel may continue.

CHEATHAM. Thank you, your honor. Members of the court – My thoughtlessly gullible clients here have seen their dreams trampled and forgotten after they paid substantial fees to a company promising them stardom. The Stardom Talent Agency took out advertisements promising everything from parts in movies to appearances at Carnegie Hall, alleging connections with unethical producers and sleazy directors and claiming to represent successful performers and artists whose names were remarkably similar to pop and movie stars. They swindled fool-heartedly innocent people into shelling out their life savings for screen tests, demo tapes and headshots and then pulled up stakes and left town. They preyed upon peoples ambitions and gave them back sorrow and betrayal. My clients want nothing more than to have their hard earned money refunded and their substantially high legal costs paid for, of course. Nothing more and nothing less.

JUDGE. Thank you for actually being brief, counselor. Perhaps Counselor Schyster will take his cue from you and leave the pontificating for the closing arguments. Mr. Schyster, your opening statement, if you please. Even though we don't

SCHYSTER. Certainly, you honor. Ladies and Gentlemen of the Jury, members of the court – I am here to represent the Stardom Talent Agency and it's proud founders (*Patting three audience members*) Shep, Moe and Curly. Perhaps you've never heard of their agency. Heck, even I never heard of their agency until I rear-ended their mobile home in the parking lot of the Spike Heels A Go-Go where they were negotiating some of their client's contracts with baseball bats. But a hundred years ago when William Morris first started, no one heard of him either. There have been more unsuccessful talent agencies than there have been successful ones and all these agencies began with unknown, no named talent. They searched high and low, signing up as many self-centered people as possible, hoping to find at least one person with enough talent to begin both their careers. Sure many people have dreams of stardom and success. But the fact remains that most of those people just plain and simply stink. Of course, that's not something anyone knows until after they've done screen tests, demo tapes and head shots. And someone has to pay for all these expenses. Just because it turns out that in reality you're nowhere as good as your ego thinks you are, it doesn't mean you're entitled to stick someone else with the tab for your folly. You gamble and you lose – you don't get your money back. It's that simple. Sure the Stardom Talent Agency took out ads on Adult internet sites, in the backs of such respected journals as The Weekly World News and posted flyers on telephone poles near public restrooms. But no one ever went knocking on these peoples doors. No one dragged them into the mobile home office just off the entrance ramp of exit 137B or forced them to do midnight screen tests at a motel against their will. To call someone a fake and a fraud because they've told you the truth about you total lack of talent amounts to nothing less than slander and libel, and that is exactly what we are countering suing those thirty people for. All together and indivdually, as a group-kind off.

(**MONDHILL** *hits the stopwatch button on his watch and shows it with glowing pride to* **JUDGE**. *She nods, disappointed.*)

JUDGE. Thank you counselor – and as much as it pains me to admit it, I do believe you've actually hit a new record for your shortest and most understandable opening statement in your entire legal career.

(**MONDHILL** *snaps his finger and she reluctantly hands him some money.*)

MONDHILL. (*to* **MONDHILL**) You still want odds on the closing arguments?

CHEATHAM. Your honor, the plaintiffs are ready to proceed with our case.

JUDGE. That's what I was afraid of. Alright, if you feel you must, call your first witness.

CHEATHAM. The plaintiffs call (*she calls an audience member up*)

(**MONDHILL** *greets the witness.*)

MONDHILL. Please place you right hand on the New Jersey State tax code and raise your left hand. Do you solemnly swear to tell the truth, something close to the truth or at least something that sounds good at the time?

JUDGE. Say yes.

(*They'll say yes.*)

MONDHILL. Please take the stand. But not very far, 'cause will need it for the next witness.

(**MONDHILL** *and the* **JUDGE** *exchange laughter.*)

JUDGE. Mondhill, sometimes you just crack me up. Well counselor?

(**CHEATHAM** *approaches*)

CHEATHAM. Mr/Ms (*whoever*), here is a copy of your sworn affidavit, just in case you've experienced any memory loss after all the drinks you've consumed this evening.

(*She hands them a "scripted answer" page.*)

SCHYSTER. Objection, your honor! Why is s/he allowed to drink and not me?

JUDGE & MONDHILL. You're sober?

CHEATHAM. Mr/Ms (*whoever*), several months ago you responded to an ad placed in the back of the National Enquirer by the Stardom Talent Agency, did you not?

(**MONDHILL** *will point out the answers on the page for the witness – "Yes"*)

CHEATHAM. And when you arrived at the arranged audition time of 1:37 Am at room 223 at the No Tell Motel on Route 17, you were greeted by those three individuals (*she points to the defendents*), were you not?

(*"Yes"*)

CHEATHAM. Isn't it true, that after your audition, those same individuals, heaped upon you praise upon praise about your talents and promised you undreamed success if you paid them in advance a sum of $500 for what they called an electronic resume and $200 for a head shot photo, as well as an additional $250 management signing fee and a $300 postage and distribution fee, all of which you paid in cash.

(*"Yes"*)

CHEATHAM. And isn't it further true that days later you received in the mail this 8mm video cassette and this out-of-focus polariod photo of yourself and that when you went back to the No Tell Motel's room 223, the room was empty and that when you called the phone number on the copy of the management contract you had received from those same individuals (*points to defendents*) you were connected with the office of the Exotic Manure Fertilizer Company. And that from that time until today, you have never received any correspondance, auditions, bookings or employment from the Stardom Talent Agency?

(*"Yes"*)

MONDHILL. (*Giving Witness the thumbs up*) You're doing great.

CHEATHAM. No further questions for this witness, your honor.

JUDGE. Thank you, Ms. Cheatham. Mr. Schyster, do you wish to cross examin?

SCHYSTER. Of course, your honor. My clients dishonor is at stake.

JUDGE. Proceed.

SCHYSTER. Mr/Ms (*whoever*) What is your talent?

(*The audience member will not know what to say.*)

MONDHILL. You're not doing great anymore.

SCHYSTER. Come, come now, don't be shy. What is your incredible talent that you wished the Stardom Talent Agency to represent you for? (*Looking at legal brief, which unfolds to an extreme extent*) Lets see, according to this brief filed on your behalf it says here that you claim you are talented as a/n (*invent anything from an opera singing bullfighter, to juggling knives while singing like Ricki Martin or performing a mime version of Gone With the Wind*).

MONDHILL. Wow. I'd like to see you perform! You know, I put myself through court officer school working part-time as stand-up comic in Lancaster, Pennsylvania. The part of the routine that they really loved best was my impressions of barnyard animals and crops – corn and then barley – sort of a one two punch.

JUDGE. Thank you, Officer Mondhill.

MONDHILL. My boll weevil had them rolling in the aisles. It went like this.

(*He starts to do an impression.* **JUDGE** *hits her gavel.* **SIMON** *dashes in, excited by* **MONDHILL**s *performance.*)

SIMON. That's masterful – pure unadulterated genius!

JUDGE. That's enough, Officer Mondhill. You are not the one on trial here. And who are you?

SIMON. Who am I? Who am I? Why, everyone knows who I am. I am a household name.

JUDGE. So is preparation H and right now you're getting to be a pain in my you know where.

SCHYSTER. Your honor, I would like to enter into evidence at this time Mr. Richard Simon – the famous syndicated entertainment critic for the Murdock Newspapers syndicate.

CHEATHAM. Objection, you honor. You can't enter a person as evidence!

SCHYSTER. Your honor, Mr. Simon is not here as a witness, but as a determinating piece of evidence to verify and substantiate the questionable declaration of the plaintiff that any talent exists to which the Stardom Talent Agency deliberately failed to promote. Mr. Simon is merely a –

JUDGE. (*Hitting gavel*) If I allow this, will you shut up?

SCHYSTER. I'll talk less.

MONDHILL. Take it – its the best plea bargain you've ever gotten out of him.

JUDGE. (*Hitting gavel*) Objection over ruled. Mondhill, please admit Mr. Simon as evidence.

Mondhill walks forward and places an evidence tag on Simon.

MONDHILL. Let the record show that Entertainment Critic Richard Simon has been admitted as evidence in the case of the class action suit against the Stardom Talent Agency docket number 32. (*To* **JUDGE**) I'm not sure we have a plastic bag big enough to contain this evidence.

JUDGE. That's okay, Mondhill, I've read some of his reviews and I don't think there's anything big enough to contain even his head. Continue, Mr. Schyster.

SCHYSTER. And now, for the jury, the court and the newly submitted evidence, I request that the witness demonstrate their professed talent.

MONDHILL. (*to witness*) That means you're on.

JUDGE. Will the plaintiff please rise?

> (**MONDHILL** *and the attorneys will get the witness to stand up and perform whatever silly thing* **SCHYSTER** *came up with – which will be very funny of course. After the applause for the plaintiff everyone turns to* **SIMON**.)

SCHYSTER. Well?

CHEATHAM. Well?

JUDGE. Well?

SIMON. Well –

> (**SIMON** *launches into a ridiculous critical review of the "performance art presentation" – which* **MONDHILL** *will disagree on – as if they were Siskill & Ebert. They*

eventually give the performance two thumbs down.)

SCHYSTER. The defense rests.

MONDHILL. The witness may step down – and quickly.

JUDGE. Ms. Cheatham, your closing statement?

CHEATHAM. Ladies and gentlemen of the jury – we may not all be stars, but at least we have our dreams. We should not reward those that exploit them. Thank you.

JUDGE. Mr. Schyster, lets see if you can beat Ms. Cheatham in brevity. Your closing statements?

SCHYSTER. Ladies and Gentlemen of the jury, (*pointing to plaintiffs*) They stink – they pay! Thank you.

Judge snaps, Mondhill hands her money.

JUDGE. Alright, ladies and gentlemen of the jury, the time has come for you to deliberate the merits of both sides of this case over the next break. I ask that you make your decision by marking your juror ballot sheet under Case 2: John Do et al Class Action VS Stardom Talent Agency. You will be deciding whether the Stardom Talent Agency is indeed guilty of fraud, misrepresentation and breech of contract or whether the plaintiffs are guilty of liable and defamation of character. Finale judgements on all cases heard tonight will be at the conclusion of the session. Thank you and good deliberating. This court will now have a short recess.

(*The* **JUDGE** *hits the gavel, everyone mingles.* **SCHYSTER** *selects a group to be his next clients and sob whenever the name F.W. Rockworth is mentioned.*)

(*If dinner theatre, the next course is served.*)

ACT III

(*Music. The* **JUDGE** *enters and talks with* **MONDHILL**.)

JUDGE. Officer Mondhill, before we reconvene I thought I might ask you a few questions. We've worked together for quite some time and I still know very little about you. I didn't know you were a Pennsylvania boy from the farm lands of Lancaster, for instance. And tonight, you seem a little different – a little more – I'm not sure if the word would be distracted or excited.

MONDHILL. Oh – yes – I'm sorry, your honor. But, well, you see it's my birthday tonight.

JUDGE. Oh, congratulations.

MONDHILL. Thank you, your honor. And, as I had to work tonight, a lot of my relatives decided to surprise me and come to court to help me celebrate.

JUDGE. Really, how sweet.

MONDHILL. Yes – you see I'm a twin – I have several identical brothers and sister – and cousins for that matter.

JUDGE. And they're here tonight? I'd love to meet them.

(**MONDHILL** *goes from birthday guest to birthday guest, introducing them to the* **JUDGE** *as his brothers, sisters and cousins – coming up with silly names and giving them outrageous occupations from landfill architecture to being a Mack truck crash test dummy, a horse shoe salesman to crop psychiatrist, billiards referee to a Hershey Chocolate Bean Safety Engineer.*)

MONDHILL. And as a special surprise they even made me my favorite cake – a rum and vodka up-side-down cake, which I think I may have eaten a little to much of.

JUDGE. Well, Officer Mondhill, you have a fascinating family. And I'd like to wish you and yours a happy birthday. (*She leads everyone in singing happy birthday*)

(*The lawyers dash in singing. As the song ends, the two attorneys pull out cards and dash to two different birthday guests.*)

LAWYERS. Age discrimination suits my specialty.

JUDGE. Speak of the devil, his disciples have arrived. Ms. Cheatham, Mr. Schyster, are you ready to reconvene?

CHEATHAM. Yes, your honor – however, as I just managed to secure a book deal for my career story from Mr. Dell Doubleday here (*pointing out a guest*) – he did both Marsha's and Johnnie's books – I was wondering if I could see if any of the fine sketches from our court artist were suitable as the jacket cover.

MONDHILL. Oh, I'm sure they are.

(**MONDHILL** *takes the sketch pad from the audience member assigned court artist earlier. This time, however,* **MONDHILL** *pulls out sketches of famous paints from the back of the pad. The last one is on velvet.* **SIMON** *runs in.*)

SIMON. A masterpiece! Such flair, such passion!

JUDGE. Officer Mondhill, please remove the previously submitted evidence Mr. Richard Simon from the courtroom.

(**MONDHILL** *begins to remove* **SIMON**.)

SIMON. You can't stifle that kind of talent. It needs to be encouraged – inspired – exhibited –

JUDGE. And you need to be expelled.

(*She hits her gavel.* **MONDHILL** *throws* **SIMON** *out the door. There is the sound of crashing outside.*)

MONDHILL. That was fun. Can I do that again? (*grabs shoulders of a near by audience member*)

JUDGE. Not right now, Officer and no more cake. I think it's time to reconvene this court.

MONDHILL. Oh – right.

(**MONDHILL** *dashes to the front of the room.*)

MONDHILL. Here yea, here yea, the Peoples Night Court is back in session, the honorable Judy Koch presiding. All sit, all be risen – I mean, all risen all's well – I mean – (*noticing Judge is already here*) – but her honor is already seated, so all be seated that ends well.

(**JUDGE** *hits her gavel.*)

JUDGE. Close enough for government work. The next case, Officer Mondhill.

SCHYSTER. Your honor, as time is getting short and my opponent has had the opportunity to press two cases, I would like –

CHEATHAM. (*Slamming table and standing up*) TWO? Two?

SCHYSTER. Yes two. That product liability case and then the class action suit –

CHEATHAM. The product liability case was thrown out!

SCHYSTER. As well it should have been! But you did get a chance to present it, so therefore it counts. Now I've only been able to present one case and –

CHEATHAM. You can't count a case that was thrown out as being presented!

SCHYSTER. Of course you can. It couldn't have been thrown out if it wasn't presented. So since you've presented two cases and I've only presented one, now it's my turn. Your honor, members of the court –

CHEATHAM. Your turn? Who do you think you are deciding it's your turn?

JUDGE. (*Slamming gavel*) Order in the court!

SCHYSTER. Pastrami on rye.

CHEATHAM. Tuna salad on toasted whole wheat.

MONDHILL. (*Writing down an order list*) I'll have a simple ham and cheese. (*To* **JUDGE**) And you?

JUDGE. The tuna salad sounds good. Now that that's taken care of, Officer Mondhill, the next case please

MONDHILL. Right. The children of F.W. Rockworth, represented by Counselor Schyster vs the estate of F.W. Rockworth, represented by Counselor Cheatham contesting the will of the late F.W.Rockworth.

JUDGE. So entered. (*Hits gavel*) As counsel for the plaintiff, Mr. Schyster will begin with opening remarks.

(*He sticks his tongue out at* **CHEATHAM**, *who sticks her tongue out back at him.*)

JUDGE. Are you ready to proceed even though we'd all wish you weren't, Mr. Schyster?

SCHYSTER. (*Scrambling to find his notes*) Not really, your honor.

JUDGE. Proceed anyway, counselor. (*Hits gavel*)

SCHYSTER. (*Not being able to find his file*) Oh – ah – well –

(**CHEATHAM** *laughs at him.*)

SCHYSTER. (*Obviously winging it*) Ah – er – Your honor, ladies and gentlemen of the jury, people of the court – – F. W. Rockworth. F. W. Rockworth. (*Not sure what else to say*) F. W. Rockworth!

MONDHILL. There were three of them?

JUDGE. We know the name of the deceased is F. W. Rockworth.

SCHYSTER. Yes – A name we all know. – ah – Who hasn't walked into an F. W. Rockworth 5 & 10 and come out with a wallet 20 to 30 dollars lighter? Uh? Right – The – ah – Rockwell stores were a part of our – culture, a part of our history, a part of our lives. So when F. W. Rockworth died last month, we all felt the loss. But – (*grasping for a thought*) but – but no one felt the loss more than his loyal loving children (*He points to a table of guests of various ages*). Yes, although still in mourning, here they sit with us tonight – all of them, sitting right here, at this table, with us tonight – from youngest to oldest – legitimate to illegitimate. Here they are, flat broke and up to their eyebrows in debt because when their money bags piggy bank father kicked-off and turned cold, he left them out in the cold too, with a surprise second Will which cut them all off from their one million dollar a year allowance. A surprise second Will signed on the same day that F.W. Rockworth leaped from his wheel chair and flung himself out of the third story window of his Bedminster estate, barely missing the estate gardener and flattening his pet bull which the gardener was taking for its morning constitutional. A surprise second Will that left F.W. Rockworth's entire 2 billion estate to his live in nurse. A surprise second Will that we shall prove was written when F.W. Rockworth was obviously not of sane state and mind and therefore must be declared to be null and void! Thank you.

(*He sits. Everyone is shocked.* **MONDHILL** *and* **JUDGE** *stare at each other, mouths open, dumbfounded.*)

JUDGE. You're finished with your opening statement?

SCHYSTER. Ah – yes your honor.

MONDHILL. You mean, you're done?

SCHYSTER. Yeah.

CHEATHAM. Objection! He can't possibly have an opening statement that short and intelligent – he's neither. (*To* **SCHYSTER**) Go on, keep talking! Rattle on for another five minutes. Say something really stupid like you usually do!

SCHYSTER. Objection, your honor. Leading the plaintiff's counsel.

JUDGE. Sustained, Mr. Schyster. Over ruled, Ms. Cheatham. Ms. Cheatham, opening statement for the defense?

CHEATHAM. (*Still in shock*) Yes – I mean, yes I have one.

JUDGE. Can we hear it then, please?

CHEATHAM. Oh – Right – I mean of course. (*Finding notes*) Ah, well, ah – I'm sorry, your honor, but the actions of opposing counsel has thrown me a little off balance.

JUDGE. As it has to us all – your opening statement, Ms. Cheatham?

CHEATHAM. Yes – Your honor, my co-counsel will present the defense's opening statement.

JUDGE. Very well.

(CHEATHAM *hands her opening statement to an audience member*)

AUDIENCE MEMBER. Your Honor, Ladies and Gentlemen of the jury, members of the court – F.W. Rockworth was a smart and industrious man who started the concept of the department store and built an empire. He was in full possession of his wits then just as he was when he wrote out his second Will and Testimony – a Will that cut out all his spoiled, uncaring, self-center, irresponsible off-spring – stopping them from living off him in death the way they had in life. Just look at them (*walks to table of plaintiffs*) Look at these faces – faces of greed, of self – indulgence, of pampered lethergy.

SCHYSTER. Objection! Counsel is using terminology the plaintiffs don't understand, much less plaintiffs counsel and probably even the defendants co-counsel. The least s/he can do is speak English.

(MONDHILL & JUDGE *turn and look at each other.*)

MONDHILL & JUDGE. He's fine.

JUDGE. Objection over-ruled.

MONDHILL. Nice to see you back to normal, Mr. Schyster.

JUDGE. Counsel for the defense may continue.

(CHEATHAM *stands and takes over for the audience member.*)

CHEATHAM. Thank you, your honor. And thank you co-counsel (*audience member's name*) Esquire. The defense will show that F. W. Rockworth always planned on having the last laugh on his scheming children and that his most recent Will was not only written while he was fully in control of his senses, but was part of his well calculated, long term plan and that there is no legal bases to have his last dying wishes ignored. Thank you.

(**CHEATHAM** *shakes her co-counselors hand before she sits down.*)

JUDGE. Mr. Schyster, I suppose you'll want to call your first witness?

SCHYSTER. (*Looking for his file*) I do? Yes, I suppose – but, I can't seem to find – –

MONDHILL. (*Whistles*) Here Witness, witness, witness! Here boy!

JUDGE. Officer Mondhill, what are you doing?

MONDHILL. Helping Mr. Schyster find his first witness. That witness has to be here somewhere.

(*to a guest*) Check your pockets. (*To another guest*) Maybe you're sitting on him. Everyone, look under your chairs.

(*Both* **SCHYSTER** *and* **CHEATHAM** *begin to help* **MOND-HILL** *look.* **JUDGE** *rolls her eyes.*)

JUDGE. (*to audience*) I don't believe this.

MONDHILL. Oo, oo, I found it – I found the plaintiffs first witness!

(**MONDHILL** *picks anyone from the audience and brings them up to the stand.*)

MONDHILL. Raise your left hand and place the hand that's left on the Campaign finance abuse handbook. Do you solemnly swear to say whatever it is your attorney tells you to say, regardless of the truth, so help you Chase Manhattan? Sure you do, sit down. Your witness, Mr. Schyster.

JUDGE. I say that, Officer Mondhill.

MONDHILL. Oh, sorry your honor.

JUDGE. Is this your witness, Counselor Schyster?

SCHYSTER. Well – I seem to have misplaced my briefs –

(**CHEATHAM** *opens her briefcase and tosses a pair of men's bikini briefs at him.*)

JUDGE. This is all more than we need to know, Counselor. Can you proceed with the case or shall I grant a finding in favor of the defendant by default?

SCHYSTER. (*Quickly approaching the witness*) Isn't true – whoever you are – that for the past few months prior to F.W. Rockworth's suicide, you observed him exhibiting eccentric behavior – unstable behavior in fact? – such as buying alien abduction insurance and making large contributions to the Dan Quayle for President campaign? Isn't it true that you witnessed F.W. Rockworth when he was delusionary, dressing up as a giant avocado and hiring the entire University of Miami's all girls swim to dress as taco chips and fill his in ground swimming pool with medium spicy salsa? Isn't it true that on the day before his unfortunate leap from his third floor window, F.W. Rockworth told you that he was secretly working with Elvis on making a come-back CD? Wouldn't you, in your expert opinion, declare Mr. F.W. Rockworth to be – how can I but this gently? – totally off his nut – and therefore anything he wrote on that day, especially a new Will and Testament – would obviously be considered not to have been written while he was in a sane state of mind? Of course you would! Thank you. No further questions your honor.

CHEATHAM. Objection!

JUDGE. Too late.

CHEATHAM. But he was leading the witness!

JUDGE. He was pulling them by a rope around the neck. But you sure took a long time in objecting, so I'll let it ride. You snooze, you lose. Do you wish to cross examine, Counselor Cheatham?

CHEATHAM. I'll say I do! My co-counsel will tear that testimony to pieces. (*Handing notes to audience member*)

JUDGE. But you are the only one listed as the defense counsel, Ms. Cheatham.

CHEATHAM. Right, I'll do it, your honor. (*To Witness*) Have you ever even met F. W. Rockworth?

(*They'll probably say "No."*)

CHEATHAM. No further questions, your honor.

MONDHILL. The witness may step down. Now, that wasn't too painful was it? I mean, if you want painful –

JUDGE. Officer Mondhill – no more rum cake.

MONDHILL. Sorry, you honor.

JUDGE. Counselor Schyster, I doubt if you have any more witnesses as you didn't really have this one, but I have to ask all the same. Does the plaintiff have any further witnesses?

SCHYSTER. Yes, your honor. Plaintiff would like to call to the stand the recipient of the majority of F.W. Rockworth's estate – his personal live-in companion, the young Nurse Ulga.

MONDHILL. Nurse Ulga? Oh, boy, this will be fun. Calling Nurse Ulga to the stand!

*(**NURSE ULGA** [the same actor as **SNITCH**/etc in wig and nurse costume] enters and walks up to **MONDHILL** to be sworn in. **MONDHILL** holds up a book, but is taken back by Ulga's ugliness.)*

MONDHILL. Ug!

NURSE. No, Ulga. Mein name is Ulga. Ulga Lubensmartzs. (*To audience member laughing the hardest*) And you look like you could do with a good enema.

(She pulls out of her pockets a pair of rubber gloves and starts putting them on.)

MONDHILL. Hey – wait – you can't wear rubber gloves when I swear you in.

NURSE. How do I know where that book's been? Um?

MONDHILL. Hey – listen lady, if you really are one. We ran out of bibles two courtrooms ago, so we're just using whatever we have left. Right now it's "My Turn" by Nancy Reagan.

NURSE. (*Removing gloves*) Oh, well I know it's alright then – as no ones ever even touched that book.

MONDHILL. Hand – Book – Hand – raise – Truth – Swear – Sit down.

SCHYSTER. Nurse Ulga, is it true that you had been F.W. Rockworth's live-in personal companion for the last two years and in his new Will he left half his estate to charity and the other half to you?

NURSE. Ja – Sure. He lovoft me.

SCHYSTER. That's proof of his insanity right there. Plaintiff rests. Your witness.

CHEATHAM. Nurse Ulga, for the past two years of your life, you were at wheel chair bound F.W. Rockworths beck and call 24 hours a day, 7 days a week, isn't that true?

NURSE. Ja – Sure. I lovoft him.

CHEATHAM. Nurse Ulga, prior to the day of his death, did any of Mr. F.W. Rockworth's children come around to visit him during his battle with his illness, over say, the past two years?

NURSE. Not a one. None of them ever came by or even called. Only their attorney, Mr. Schyster, would call and ask "Is he dead yet?" and I'd say no and he'd hang up.

CHEATHAM. You're sure? You're sure that in the two years that F.W. Rockworth was suffering from a terminal disease, (*Walking to "relatives"*) not one of these individuals ever came to visit their father?

NURSE. They never even came to the funeral. Rocky, he would tell me about his no good, money grubbing, bloodsucking, circling vulture off-spring, and show me their pictures, every time he had a new witch doctor flown in from some strange country to place a curse on their heads. He said the only time I'd ever see them is when they'd take me to court to contest his Will.

CHEATHAM. He knew they'd contest his will?

NURSE. Ja – sure. That's why he waited until the last day before he died to write his real Will. He knew the day would come that the pain would get too much and he could no longer bear being confined like a prisoner to that wheel chair, oxygen tank, intravenous and nuclear powered pacemaker – taking that medicine that just prolonged his – and everyone else's agony – and that he'd throw himself out the third floor window, aiming for the gardener's nasty little dog – which he got. Splat! Rocky had the last laugh, Ja – died with a smile on his face, he did (*to herself*) – the only smile I ever saw on the dirty old fart –

(**CHEATHAM** *clears her throat – as a signal to* **NURSE**.)

NURSE. (*Notices* **CHEATHAM**) – I mean loving old man.

CHEATHAM. Did any of his children ever send him anything?

NURSE. Oh, Ja – sure. (*Pointing to "relatives"*) That one sent him a bushel of juicy exotic fruits – which had scorpion nests in them. Would never have known until it was too late if it wasn't for the cooks drunken ex-boyfriend breaking in and getting stung to death by the little critters. And that one sent him a delicious banana coffee cake, which the gardener ate, which was good cause Rocky was allergic to nuts and that cake was full of them – all ground up so you wouldn't notice. And that one sent him an exotic pet – a giant Amazon python – which turned out to be poisonous. And That one sent him a nice little gun with a note, "Better to end it sooner than later."

CHEATHAM. Thank you, Nurse Ugla. You've been most helpful. No further questions, your honor.

SCHYSTER. Wait – wait – Your honor, Plaintiff would like to re-dress the witness.

NURSE. Oh, that sounds like fun – you naughty boy.

MONDHILL. That just means he wants to ask you another question.

NURSE. Oh.

JUDGE. You may approach the witness, Counselor Schyster.

SCHYSTER. I may, but I don't want to. I'll ask my question from here. Nurse Ulga, if F.W. Rockworth was so ill that he was wheelchair bound, on the day he wrote this new Will, how did he manage to lift himself up and throw himself out a third floor window?

NURSE. (*Caught off guard*) Well – I – I don't know. But even the invalid can do amazing things when they put their minds to it. Maybe he got an extra lift from the high fiber Wheaties he ate that morning.

SCHYSTER. He got an extra lift alright – from you!

CHEATHAM. Objection, your honor. Nurse Ulga isn't the one on trial here.

JUDGE. Sustained. Strike that last statement from the record. The witness may step down.

NURSE. (*Winking to audience man as she exits*) And I'll see you for a physical later, big boy.

JUDGE. Any further witnesses, Counselor Schyster? Counselor Cheatham? No? Good! The plaintiff may present closing arguments.

SCHYSTER. Closing arguments – right. Ladies and Gentlemen of the jury, look at these grieving faces, suffering from having lost a reclusive and unresponsive father. You heard testimony of how, even though neglected and forbidden to visit, they continued to send thoughtful presents to their patriarch, who was being turned against them by this vixen woman (*he is repulsed by Nurse Ulga*) Ugh – who saw in F.W. Rockworth only a pay check and a billion dollar piggy bank. Certainly we can not allow a hastily, obviously dictated, false will written at a moment of painful insanity, to take from these loving children their only mementos of their beloved father – and take from me a whopping one third contingency fee. NO! Justice must be done – and I need that vacation house in Aruba. Thank you.

MONDHILL. Oh, Aruba's very nice this time of year. Judge, did you know why they call it Aruba?

JUDGE. Actually, no Officer Mondhill – why did they name it Aruba?

MONDHILL. Well – they call it Aruba because Pittsburgh was taken. (*Laughs at his own joke*).

JUDGE. Counselor Cheatham, defenses closing arguments.

CHEATHAM. Ladies and Gentlemen of the jury. Here is a clear case of a family of heartless, uncaring relatives that eagerly awaited the death of their wealthy father, only to find that because of their coldness, they've been cut out. So what if F.W. Rockworth left half his billion dollar estate to his homely nurse. At least she was there for him, for two years. Who are we to take away his final wishes, and my very large estate management fee? I need that vacation condo in St. Martin. Thank you.

MONDHILL. Oh, St. Martin! That's nice too. That's the island that has two sides. One side is French, the other toast. (*Laughs*) I'm killing myself.

JUDGE. Well, you're maiming us, Mondhill. Alright, ladies and gentlemen of the jury, the time has come for you to deliberate the merits of both sides of this case over the next break. I ask that you make your decision by marking your juror ballot sheet for Case 3: Children of F.W. Rockworth VS Estate of F.W. Rockworth and then hand the competed ballot sheet in to Officer Mondhill as soon as possible. You will be deciding whether you feel Mr. Rockworth was competent when he authored his revised Will, cutting out his children and leaving half his estate to charity and the other half to his nurse or whether he was mentally unbalanced and thus reinstate his previous Will, splitting his fortune equally among his children and leaving nothing to his employees – including his nurse. Finale judgements on all cases heard tonight will be at the conclusion of the session. Thank you and good deliberating. This court will now have a short recess.

(*The* **JUDGE** *hits the gavel and the next course is served. The two attorneys walk around and attempt to persuade the jurors.* **MONDHILL** *collects all the ballots and tabulates them.*)

(*If dinner theatre, the next course is served.*)

ACT IV

(Music from ABC's Wide World of Sports plays. **HOWARD COSTAR, JR** *– a sportscaster dressed in a blazer, enters with a hand held microphone.)*

HOWARD. Good evening ladies and gentlemen and welcome back to ABC's Wide World of Court. I'm your host Howard Costar Jr, talking to you live from the floor of Judge Judy's Peoples Night Court, where the jury has been deliberating and is about to come back with their verdicts. It's been a wild ride tonight, with an action packed rematch between Counselor Sydney Schyster of Springer, Schyster and Shark and Counselor Melissa Cheatham of Dewy, Cheatham and Howe. Oh, and here come the contenders now, walking back into the ring and their respective corners.

(The music from Peter Gunn plays as both lawyers enter with towels around their necks and sipping from water bottles. They both joggle about a little like boxers, then start dancing in unison.)

HOWARD. The tension is high tonight as we round the corner to the finish in this brutal contest of wits, guts and utter bull. A lot is riding on this moment – the moment of truth or consequences, the moment of win, lose or draw, the moment of who wants to be a millionaire. Lets move down to the crowd and get some honest comments from the loyal fans.

(During **HOWARD**'*s last lines, both lawyers give signs and pom poms to audience members on their sides of the room.* **HOWARD** *moves to an audience member with a "Go Schyster Go" sign.)*

HOWARD. I see you're a Schyster fan. How do you think your man has faired tonight in this battle of the sexes? Is he coming out on top or is he whipped?

(*Who knows what they'll say.*)

HOWARD. Well, I know your money's riding on him and I wouldn't want to be in your shoes. Now, lets move on over to some fans of the competition.

(**HOWARD** *goes to an audience member with a sign "Cheatam All The Way."*)

HOWARD. Wow, what a night. I see you've brought an entire cheering section with you. So, how to you think you're favorite is going to fair this evening? Will she come up roses or be pushing up the daisies?

(*Who knows what they'll say.*)

HOWARD. Well, you can tell you were a Marcia Clarke fan and look what happened to her. But good luck and I hope you didn't risk too much. Oh, wait, here's the court office Duke Mondhill. – A tense hush is falling over the court. It looks like this might be it. Ladies and Gentlemen.

(**JUDGE** *enters.*)

MONDHILL. Here yea, here yea, this session of the Peoples Night Court is now back in session, Her honorable Judge Judy Koch presiding. All be receded.

(**JUDGE** *hits the gavel.*)

JUDGE. Thank you, Officer Mondhill. Well, before we get to the golden moments here, do you want to raise the stakes or are you changing your mind now that the nights through?

MONDHILL. What – change my mind? Cheatham held her own, no question. Right folks?

(*He gets them to cheer.*)

JUDGE. Held? You have to do more than hold, Mondhill. Schyster started out strong and ended with a flourish. Right folks?

(*She gets them to cheer.*)

MONDHILL. Flourish – he forgot he was even representing that last case!

JUDGE. Which explains why he did so well. Double or nothing?

MONDHILL. You got it, Judge!

(*They shake and throw down money.* **JUDGE** *hits that gavel.*)

JUDGE. This court will now come to order.

ALL. I'll have –

(*She slams the gavel.*)

JUDGE. We've exhausted that joke. Now, have the Juries come to their verdicts?

MONDHILL. They have your honor.

JUDGE. Every well. Would the jury foreman in the case of Fangdangelmen vs Guffman, please rise?

(**MONDHILL** *picks person from the audience and hands them the jury tabulation sheet.*)

MONDHILL. How does the jury find?

FOREMEN. We the jury find the defendant Doctor Guffman (*Guilty/not guilty*) as charged and award damages and compensation to (*The plaintiff/the defendant*).

(*Which ever side wins hoots and hollers. The* **JUDGE** *pounds the gavel.*)

JUDGE. So entered into the records of this court. Would the jury foreman in the case of Peoples Class Action Suit vs The Stardom Talent Agency please rise?

(**MONDHILL** *picks another jury foreman to stand.*)

MONDHILL. How does the jury find?

FOREMEN. We the jury find the defendant Stardom talent Agency (*Guilty/not guilty*) as charged and award damages and compensation to (*The plaintiff/the defendant*).

(*Which ever side wins hoots and hollers. The* **JUDGE** *pounds the gavel.*)

JUDGE. So entered into the records of this court. Would the jury foreman in the case of The Children of F.W. Rockworth VS the Estate of F.W. Rockworth please rise?

(**MONDHILL** *picks another jury foreman to stand.*)

MONDHILL. How does the jury find?

FOREMEN. We the jury find that F.W. Rockworth was fully (*Sane/Insane*) at the time of the writing of his new Will and therefore find in favor of (*The plaintiff/the defendant*).

(**JUDGE** *hits gavel.*)

JUDGE. So entered into this court of record.

MONDHILL. That makes _______ for Schyster and _______ for Cheatham. Counselor ___________ is our winner tonight!

(*Triumphant music plays. The* **JUDGE** *and* **MONDHILL** *exchange money on the bet and shake. The two attorneys walk forward and shake hands. They shake hands with the* **JUDGE**. **MONDHILL** *places a winners wreath on the winner and shakes hands.* **HOWARD** *dashes up to the winner.*)

HOWARD. Wow! What a win, what a competition! Congratulations!

WINNER. Thank you, thank you. I'd like to thank all the little people – (*pointing to audience members*) There's her over there – and him over there and oh, yes, her and –

HOWARD. Enough of the small talk, when did you know you had it in the bag – when you knew the glove wouldn't fit –

WINNER. Well – I –

HOWARD. Fascinating! (*Dashing to defeated attorney*) When did you know it was over? When you felt like that deer, caught in the headlights – that mouse in the trap – like McCain in the primaries?

LOSER. Well – I –

HOWARD. Fascinating! Lets move on to the judge – Judge Judy – do you have any final words?

JUDGE. Yes – court is adjourned.

(*She exits.*)

HOWARD. Well, that sounds finale to me.

CHEATHAM. Well, darling, well done.

SCHYSTER. No, it was you that was spectacular – as always.

CHEATHAM. Aren't you just the sweetest? Shall we go home?

(*They begin to exit.*)

SCHYSTER. I thought you might want to stop in for a midnight snack at that all night St. Martin restaurant – French Toast!

CHEATHAM. Oh, and then we can stop off at that new place opened up right next door – what was the name?.

SCHYSTER. The trauma emergency room!

BOTH. New Clients!

(*They kiss.*)

MONDHILL. This session of the Peoples Night Court has concluded, court is dismissed.

(*He starts to straighten up.*)

HOWARD. Wow! Well, there you have it – and there it is. So, as we say in legal land, let all your briefs be snug, all your files be emery and all your suits be three piece. Good night, and good luck in court!

(*They all exit to Perry Mason Music. Black Out. Curtain call.*)

OPENING STATEMENT

Your Honor, Ladies and Gentlemen of the jury, members of the court – F.W. Rockworth was a smart and industrious man who started the concept of the department store and built an empire. He was in full possession of his wits then just as he was when he wrote out his second Will and Testimony – a Will that cut out all his spoiled, uncaring, self-centered, irresponsible off-spring – stopping them from living off him in death the way they had in life. Just look at them (walks to table of plaintiffs) Look at these faces – faces of greed, of self-indulgence, of pampered lethargy.

JURY FORM

We, the jury, find the defendant ________________
Guilty/not guilty
as charged and award damages to
(Name of person that won)

JURY BALLOT

Case 1
I find in favor of ____

Case 2
I find in favor of ____

Case 3
I find in favor of ____

PROPS

Gavel
Steno pad
Sketch pad
Frankenstein photo
Mona Lisa, the Scream, Whistler's Mother (copies)
Evidence tag
Dockets (at least 4)
Legal papers
Briefcases (2 – one for each attorney)
Water bottles & straws (2)
Towels (2)
Hand Held Microphone
Money (for Mondhill & Judge)
Cup of take out coffee
Men's briefs (for Cheatham to give to Schyster)

Also by
David Landau & Nikki Stern...

The Altos

Murder at Café Noir

Murderous Crossings

Noir Suspicious

Please visit our website **samuelfrench.com** for complete
descriptions and licensing information